The School Play

Text and jacket art by

Rosemary Wells

Interior illustrations by

Jody Wheeler

VOLO

Hyperion Books for Children
New York

Printed in the United States of America

First Edition
3 5 7 9 10 8 6 4 2

LIBRARY OF CONGRESS CATALOGING-IN-PUBLICATION DATA
Wells, Rosemary.
The school play / Rosemary Wells.
p.   cm.— (Yoko and friends—school days ; 2)
Summary: When Yoko's class puts on a play about taking care of teeth, not
everyone is happy with their part.
ISBN 0-7868-0721-0 (hardcover)—ISBN 0-7868-1527-2 (pbk.)
[1. Cats—Fiction. 2. Kindergarten—Fiction. 3. Schools—Fiction. 4. Theater—
Fiction. 5. Teeth—Care and hygiene—Fiction.] I. Title.
PZ7.W46843Sc   2001
[E]—dc21   00-57261

Visit www.hyperionchildrensbooks.com

"Good morning, boys and girls!"

said Mrs. Jenkins.

"Good morning, Mrs. Jenkins!"

said everyone.

Everyone held hands in a circle

and sang the "Good Morning" song.

"Good morning on my left!

Good morning on my right!

May our day be filled with play

Until the stars come out tonight!"

"Today, boys and girls," said
Mrs. Jenkins, "we will choose
the roles for our class play!"
"I want to be the queen!" said Doris.

"We're going to be Frankenstein!"
said the Franks.

"There is no queen and no
Frankenstein in this play,"
said Mrs. Jenkins.

"Our play is about keeping our
teeth strong and clean.
Now, who wants to play the part
of the dentist?"

Claude raised his hand and said,

"Me! Me! Me!"

Timothy got to be the toothbrush.

Doris was the dental floss.

Nora was the toothpaste.

Grace was the bottle of mouthwash.

One Frank was a Caramel Clump Chocolate Bar.

The other Frank was a wisdom tooth.

And Yoko was a cavity.

Everyone went home learning the lines for the play.

Everyone went home happy, except Yoko.

Yoko played her violin.

But the music sounded so sad that

her mother asked,

"What's the matter, my little

cherry blossom?"

10

"I am only a cavity in the school play," said Yoko.

"Surely the cavity does something interesting," said Yoko's mother.

"No," said Yoko. "The cavity just sits there.

"Then the Caramel Clump Chocolate Bar gets on top and says, 'I am stuck here forever!' After that, the dentist puts a filling in me."

"Well, I will make you the best cavity costume anyone has ever seen," said Yoko's mother.

At play practice, the class chairs were set in a half circle. "They look like a mouth full of teeth," said Timothy.

Yoko asked Nora if she would like to trade being the toothpaste for being a cavity.

"No," said Nora. "I don't want to be an old cavity. The cavity doesn't say a word!"

Claude wouldn't trade, either.

Neither would Doris or Grace or

anyone else.

No one wanted to be the cavity.

"Come, Yoko," said Mrs. Jenkins,
"time to sit in your chair.
Claude, are you ready to put in
the filling?"

"I am ready," said Claude.

"What do you have behind your
back, Claude?" asked Mrs. Jenkins.

"It's my father's drill,"

said Claude.

"It makes a perfect noise."

"You can't use tools in the play,

Claude," said Mrs. Jenkins.

"I am sure you can make excellent

drill noises by yourself."

"It's no fun to be the dentist if I can't use my drill," said Claude. "If we use our imaginations, we can all be happy with our parts in the play," said Mrs. Jenkins.

Every morning, Mrs. Jenkins called
a play practice.

Every morning, Claude complained.

"I don't want to make buzzing

noises. I want to use my father's

drill," said Claude.

Thursday afternoon, on the school
bus, Timothy said, "You look
unhappy, Yoko."

"I don't like being an old cavity,"
said Yoko.

"Who would?" said Timothy.

"What's in the suitcase?" Timothy
asked.

"My violin," said Yoko.

"Can I see it?" Timothy asked.

Yoko showed him.

"Can I try it?"

Yoko let him.

But she had to put her hands over
her ears.

"Stop that noise!" said everyone
on the bus.

"You know what?" asked Timothy.

"What?" said Yoko.

"The violin sounds just like a
dentist's drill!"

Timothy plucked the strings.

"I love it! I want to do it again!"

he said.

"I have an idea," said Yoko.

Yoko and her mother made her

cavity costume.

Yoko painted a box black.

Yoko's mother made a

white tooth top.

On Friday morning, all the mamas
and daddies came to the school
and sat in their seats.

The curtain opened.

The play began.

Timothy came out holding his

toothbrush.

He dipped into Nora's toothpaste
and brushed every tooth up and
down. Doris flossed between the
teeth with a string.

Grace sprayed blue mouthwash
into the air.

Then Frank, the Caramel Clump

Bar, came on.

He sat right on top of Yoko's

tooth box.

"I am stuck here forever!" said

Frank.

The lights went out. The spotlight

went on.

The dentist came in. Claude
pulled Caramel Frank from the
tooth with his dental cleaning tool.
"This candy bar has made
a terrible hole in the tooth.
Now I must drill it and fill it," said
Claude. *"Buzz Buzz."*

Suddenly from inside the cavity box came the most awful drilling noise.

ZIN ZIN ZIZZ ZIZZ WOWEEEEE Zeeeee!

Claude did not know what had happened.

The lights went on.

All the mamas and daddies

clapped and cheered.

They asked for the drill again and

again and one more time.

Everyone took a bow.

And Yoko came out fiddling!

Dear Parents,

When our children were young we lived in a small house, but we always made a space just for books. When their dad or I would read a story out loud, the TV was always off—radio and music, too—because it intruded.

Soon this peaceful half hour of every day became like a little island vacation. Our children are lifetime readers now with an endless curiosity for the rich world waiting between the covers of good books. It cost us nothing but time well spent and a library card.

This set of easy-to-read books is about the real nitty-gritty of elementary school. There are new friends, and bullies, too. There are germs and the "Clean Hands" song, new ways of painting pictures, learning music, telling the truth, gossiping, teasing, laughing, crying, separating from Mama, scary Halloweens, and secret valentines. The stories are all drawn from the experiences my children had in school.

It's my hope that these books will transport you and your children to a setting that's familiar, yet new. And that it will prove to be a place where you can explore the exciting new world of school together.

Rosemary Wells